Caramel Addiction

Chocolate Caramel Vanilla, Volume 1

Shaun J. Phree

Published by PLE Press LLC, 2020.

Also by Shaun J. Phree

Chocolate Caramel Vanilla
Caramel Addiction
Vanilla Fetish
Chocolate Obsession

Nu Nu Lambda
Soror Love

Standalone
No Love Lost: A Poetic Tale
10 Steps to Self Care
Her Mother, My Love
Never
Writer's Surge
Classified

Table of Contents

Chapter One

"Stop, Qing!" Jade giggled, falling off the couch and running from Persia's tickling attack.

"Not until you say it. You know how this goes! SAY IT!" Persia laughed.

"Okay!" Persia fell back on the couch to give Jade a chance to comply with her request. Jade continued, "I love you more than ever before, I love you more than my heart can store, and I will love you every day more and more. You happy now." Jade pouted on the floor.

Persia picked Jade up onto the couch and held her. "You are my heart; you are my breath; without you, I would have nothing left." Persia passionately kissed Jade. They made love that night as if it was the last time. Their love felt brand new each time they touched each other.

TWO YEARS AGO, PERSIA fell in love with Jade the first time she laid eyes on her at a Halloween party. Her beautiful caramel skin, perfect curves, and radiant smile took Persia's breath away. Every time the music started to play, Jade's body would sway to the rhythm and hypnotize Persia. They danced and intertwined their souls together. Life seemed to give them obstacles each time they tried to get together, but Persia was persistent. After taking every

chance she had to get to know Jade better, things finally clicked at a community event while volunteering. Persia wasn't going to let Jade slip through her fingers again. She was aggressive, and within a week, Persia and Jade were officially dating and moved quickly. Thirteen months later, Jade and Persia were sure of their forever and moved in together.

"GOOD MORNING, MY BEAUTIFUL Queen," Persia kissed Jade.

"Good morning, my handsome Qing," Jade returned the affection. Persia attempted to get out of bed but was pulled back. Jade jumped and straddled Persia with that look on her face. The 'you're not going anywhere until you satisfy me' look.

"My Queen, you know I have to go to work." Persia's words and hands squeezing Jade's naked ass had conflicting intentions. Jade didn't pay attention to the resistance Persia put up. It never mattered what Persia had to do; if Jade wanted to feel her...it was going to happen.

"Okay, Papi," Jade smirked. "What am I supposed to do about this?" She slid Persia's hand into her wet panties.

Dammit. I'm going to be late. Persia flipped Jade onto the bed and kissed every inch of her body. Inhaling her was the only reason she would be late for anything. She lifted Jade's body onto her shoulders and began her breakfast. Jade rode Persia's face to orgasm...twice.

"You know, it would be so much easier if we could disappear together for a year, and maybe I would get you out of my system. Until then, you'll have to keep her satisfied because she just can't get enough." Jade cooed as she looked down at the moisture between her legs.

"Why would you ever want to get me out of your system, My Love?" Persia laughed. She pulled Jade by her legs and positioned herself to have another serving of Jade's honey. Jade jumped back and cupped herself.

"No, you are going to be late, Persia. You know how you hate being late!" Jade exclaimed.

"I'm already late," Persia nuzzled her face between her lover's legs, kissing her inner thighs. "Don't act like you are concerned with me being on time now." Persia teased Jade's pearl with her tongue. "And you started this, so now I have to finish it."

Jade wrapped her legs around Persia's neck and rode her tongue to another orgasm. If they kept this up, no one would make it to work.

"Okay! I'm done. I'm so sorry, Papi, for starting it, and I know I can't finish it." Jade pleaded. She didn't mean it, but it was the only way to get Persia to stop. Otherwise, they could go on for hours.

"You're lucky I have to get to work." Persia threatened. She slowly backed away from Jade and moved towards the bathroom. She could still smell her lover's nectar on her face and was encouraged to return, but she knew work was a priority.

"Papi, the girls are going out tonight!" Jade requested permission from the bedroom. "I won't be out late, okay?"

"Don't leave me here alone too long... I might have to find something to keep me company." Persia teased. Jade slowly swayed into the bathroom and hugged Persia from behind.

"Play with me if you want to. I will gut you like a fish." Jade's sweet face, beautiful full lips, and short stature didn't take away from her threat. Jade's violent side turned Persia on. She turned around and wrapped her arms around Jade's waist.

"My Queen, you are the sweetest thing I have ever tasted. Nothing can compare to that caramel between those thighs." Persia assured her.

"My Qing." Jade stood on her toes, kissed Persia softly, and walked away. "You better know it."

Persia rushed to shower and get dressed for work. Jade was downstairs in the kitchen but left her phone on their bed. The notifications were constant, and they caught Persia's attention and stopped her journey to the shower. *Who could be messaging this early in the morning?* She typed in the four-digit security code. *Incorrect?* Jade changed her code. The two vowed never to hide anything and shared passwords for everything. *Facebook Messenger, huh?* She typed in a different four-digit code. *Incorrect!*

"Babe!!" Persia yelled, slowly walking towards Jade. "Did you change your phone security code?"

"Um, yes." Jade stalled. "Are you in the shower yet? You're going to be late."

Persia dropped her towel and headed to the stairs. Jade met her.

"Do you want me to join you?" Jade asked as she swayed her body in front of Persia.

"I went to check your phone because your messenger notifications were going off. What's your code?" Persia held Jade's phone in one hand and nudged Jade away from her with the other. Jade reached for the phone instead, but Persia pulled back.

"Can I check my phone since it's going off?" Jade asked sarcastically. Persia slowly handed Jade the phone and stood waiting while Jade unlocked it. She typed in a completely new code.

"Who is it?" Persia inquired.

Jade pressed her body against her lover's firm, naked body. "You didn't answer my question. Do you want me to join you?"

"Who is in your messenger, my Queen?" Persia asked again.

"I'm standing in front of you...like this...and you are asking about my phone?" Jade attempted to turn the focus to Persia. "Damn."

"Yes. Especially since you are trying to distract me from my question." Persia walked away, heading towards the second bathroom, but not before snatching two towels out of the closet. She answered Jade with her silence. It was better this way. She needed time to collect her thoughts before continuing.

Persia allowed every scenario to run through her mind as the scalding hot water ran over her tired muscles. This place in her mind was too familiar. By the time she got out of the shower, her mind was clear and ready to confront the situation rationally... or so she thought.

"I ALREADY TOLD YOU!" Jade yelled.

"You didn't tell me shit. You just keep giving me the runaround." Persia responded. "Who the fuck was on your phone?"

"It was just my cousin. She always messages me on FB, you know that." Jade explained.

"Let me see..." Persia requested. She was fully dressed and ready to walk out the door. She attempted to resolve this with a conversation, but Jade was defensive.

"If you don't trust me, then why are we even together? I'm tired of this. It's like we haven't proved ourselves to each other." Jade said.

"Just like I thought." Persia picked up her cell phone, briefcase, and coffee before heading silently out the door.

"Your thoughts always go there, and I'm not going to keep indulging you. You and your suspicion can sleep in the guest room tonight." Jade responded angrily before slamming the front door.

Jade always had a problem committing to Persia consistently. They have been in and out of different types of relationships over the last two years. Monogamy just didn't seem to be a viable option for the couple. Even when they were in a monogamous relationship, there was always someone Jade couldn't let go of. Persia came to terms with who Jade really was even when Jade couldn't admit it to herself. They maintained an open relationship with extremely specific rules. Jade broke the rules. Jade always broke the rules. She always had a reason. Like that made a difference.

PERSIA SAT IN SILENCE behind the wheel of her car for 5 minutes. She put her wireless headphones in her ear and said, "Call Lexi." She started her car and pulled out of the parking lot as the phone rang in her ear.

"Well, well, well...I've missed you." A seductive voice answered.

"Are you busy tonight, Lexi?" Persia asked.

"Of course not. Well, not too busy for you... What's wrong?" Lexi responded.

"Life is getting to me, and I need to see you. Tonight, your place?" Persia asked.

"For you both?" Lexi held her breath for the answer.

"No, Lexi. This time, it'll just be me." Persia said. "I just need someone to talk to. You know what I need."

"Zaddi, you know you're the only one I need and want. I don't care how many lovers you take on...I don't need anyone else. Just you. So, come over tonight when you get off work, and we will talk about anything else you want, okay?" Lexi assured.

"Should I let Jade know?

"No. You just worry about getting ready." Persia said.

"Ok, Zaddi." Lexi agreed.

Persia sat at a red light and stared at herself in the rear-view mirror. She pulled up a cash transfer app on her phone. She transferred $450 to Lexi and looked back at herself in the rear-view mirror. She smiled at herself and pulled off to start her day.

Chapter Two

Lexi laid back on the spa table and allowed her thoughts to remove her. Brazilian wax hurt. She ran through her outfit options for the night. Persia didn't like the naked look but loved a bit of sexuality. Lexi decided on no cleavage but lots of legs. Persia loved it when Lexi wore heels 5 inches or taller. She said they made her beautiful chocolate legs shine. As the technician moved on to her legs, Lexi ran through the best options for dinner. Persia only wanted home-cooked meals from Lexi; they rarely ate out. Steak is her favorite, and it will take a while to marinate. The technician finished the last part of Lexi's body.

"Ok, miss, we are done." The blonde technician assured Lexi. Her eyes lingered on Lexi until their eyes met. "Is there anything else I can do for you today?"

Lexi could feel the heat between them, but she was focused on Persia today. She sat up and allowed her towel to fall to her waist. Lexi fingered the technician's name tag that read *Ashli*, and the technician slowly toggled between her eyes and her perky chocolate nipples.

"Ashli, you did a great job. Thank you. I will be sure to request you for my next appointment. Hopefully, I will have more time to chat." Lexi flirted before standing up without her towel, leaving her completely naked. The technician took in every inch of Lexi's body before responding.

"It is my pleasure. I look forward to your next appointment." Ashli smiled and left the room.

After Lexi left the spa, she went to the grocery store and a lingerie boutique. She bought something new for Persia every time they met. Usually, they met for a threesome, but from time to time, Persia requested her company privately. Lexi picked out a piece that had a mix of black leather and lace, perfect for her evening.

"Welcome home, Ms. Sims," the doorman greeted Lexi as the driver opened her door. He immediately went for the bags showing out of the open car trunk.

"Thank you, William." Lexi waited for the doorman to follow her with her bags.

"Are we expecting Ms. Jefferson this evening?" William asked as they entered the elevator. He scanned the familiar collection of shopping bags.

"Yes, William. Please make sure security is aware so she doesn't have any problems like last time." Lexi requested.

"Consider it done, Ms. Sims." They both exited the elevator and walked down the hallway toward Lexi's apartment. She pulled her keys out of her purse, and her phone started vibrating.

"Hello," she answered as she opened her front door. She knew who was on the other end.

"Hi, Lexi," Jade responded.

"How can I help you?" She rarely spoke to Jade. William followed Lexi into the living room and followed her hand as she pointed. He settled her bags on the couch.

"I love how direct you are. If Persia calls you this afternoon, tell her you are busy." Jade commanded.

"Well, Jade, I am busy tonight; thanks for asking." Lexi snapped back while rummaging through her purse. Jade took a deep breath that could be heard on the line.

"I have something special planned for her tonight," Jade responded.

"I am busy this evening. If Persia calls this afternoon to make plans with me...well, I already have plans." Lexi said. She gave William his tip and silently thanked him before closing her front door.

"Enjoy your evening, Lexi," Jade responded.

"You as well, Jade. Goodbye." Lexi hung up the phone and headed to the kitchen. She began preparing dinner and laughed at Jade in her head. If only she knew Lexi was the first call Persia made this morning. *Persia couldn't let me go, even if she put her mind to it. Her heart and her body would veto that decision every time.*

Persia and Lexi met at a party as teenagers. There were a lot of texts and video chats until Lexi invited Persia to a festival with her friends. Their connection was instant passion. They couldn't keep their hands off each other. The electricity in their conversations translated flawlessly into their physical attraction. Persia couldn't indulge enough in Lexi's beautiful milk chocolate body. After the festival, Persia went back to the hotel with Lexi and her friends. The group booked a room for the night. Although everyone knew Persia was invited, there was a bit of thickness in the air as if one of the friends was interested in Lexi and jealous. Persia figured their hookup in the third seat of the SUV on the way to the festival wasn't the best first impression on the friends, especially the jealous one. Nothing could have ruined their night together. They spent the night swimming, talking, making love, and watching the sun rise over the city. They wrapped into each other in a monogamous relationship for three months before things changed. They both were on the cliff of major life changes that pulled them in different directions. Persia never really let Lexi go. They went on to other relationships and living life but always found their way back to each other. They started an open relationship that evolved when Persia met Jade. Persia began inviting Jade to their dates and was courting Jade and Lexi for a closed triad relationship. Jade wasn't interested in Lexi. She was comfortable with their arrangement. Lexi and Persia maintained their relationship throughout Jade and Persia's off-and-on relationship. Lexi didn't need anyone other than Persia, so she was committed only to her. They invited a third woman into their bedroom from time to time. Persia took particularly good care of Lexi even after she moved in with Jade. Persia believed it was her responsibility to take care of her lovers financially as well as spiritually, emotionally, and physically. She maintained Lexi's basic household bills and gave gifts frequently. Lexi had the freedom and space she required but was still in love with the person she planned to spend her life with.

LEXI HUNG UP THE PHONE. She lit candles all over her apartment, kept dinner warm in the kitchen, and complemented her dress with her lingerie. She was excited to see what Persia had planned for the evening. She was making the final touches to her makeup when she heard the knock at her door. A smile spread across her face, and butterflies filled her belly.

"TWENTY MINUTES, P!" Karen yelled into Persia's office.

"Damn, Karen." Persia rubbed her ears. Karen stood, rolling her eyes at her dramatic response.

"P, come on and wrap it up. It's time to go." Karen said.

"I know, I'm coming. I have plans tonight, too." Persia baited Karen. She was Persia's work best friend and was nosey as hell.

"Sweet times with the wifey, uh?" Karen fished.

"Not the wifey," Persia smirked.

"Ohhhhhhhh!!!" Karen jumped into the chair in front of Persia's desk. Persia acted like she was involved in the paperwork on her desk. Karen smacked the desk. "A LOVER!!!"

"I have a date with Lexi tonight," Persia responded without enthusiasm.

"Oh, the wife, wife, huh?" Karen leaned back in the chair, chuckling. Karen was familiar with Lexi and Persia's past. She met Lexi quite a few times since she came to Persia's office, more frequently than Jade. "You know, I think she is much more attentive and into you; I think you should invest more into her."

"Our setup is good, and everyone is happy, including me." Persia started explaining while watching the disbelief on Karen's face. "You know she doesn't want to live with anyone unless she is being carried across the threshold as a wife to her new family home. Jade and I are open to having relationships with other people, and we live together. I take care of all the financial responsibility for both of the apartments. I am in love with both, and they are in love with me." She picked up a pile of papers and headed toward her file cabinet.

"Do they date other people?" Karen asked. She never asked that before.

"Lexi doesn't want anyone else. Our relationship gives her the room to go to school, climb her corporate ladder, and run her business. Jade has a boyfriend, and I think she's still messing with her fem submissive." Persia responded while filing her paperwork. She made her way back to her desk. Karen's interested gaze followed her around the room.

"So, what about Ashli with an i?" Karen said in a valley girl's voice, mocking Persia's third lover, Ashli.

"Oh, me and Ashli...that's only about sex. That thick piece of white chocolate is a freak, and I'm addicted to trying to find something she hasn't tried. That woman is like cocaine." Persia wiped her lip like she was drooling.

"For real? I wouldn't have guessed it." Karen was confused. Ashli looked as vanilla as they came.

"Don't get me wrong, me and Lexi...that's the best sex with emotional connections. Me and Ashli, that's just the rawest, most free, and transcending sex I have ever had. I mean, lil mama got skills." Persia picked up her briefcase and jacket and headed out of her office.

"Damn, so are you ever going to settle down with just one woman?" Karen followed behind Persia.

"Honestly, I don't know. I mean, I could if it were right, but I don't see it now. I'm not ready to get married yet anyway. Jade is my heart, Lexi is my breath, and Ashli is the fire in my loins." Persia said as she started mimicking the Joker when talking about Ashli. It was a good thing they were in the elevator alone. The elevator doors opened, and Karen backed out.

"Shut up, P. You just like having your cake and eating it too." Karen laughed as they walked towards their cars.

"I like cake," Persia laughed. "No, but really, Karen, I would be happy if I could have Lexi and Jade in the same home. Those two...they don't want that."

"I don't know any woman that wants another woman in their home with their man." Karen laughed as she put her briefcase and coat in the trunk of her car.

"I've met a few, but none that matched with me," Persia responded after putting her belongings into her back seat. "I will see you tomorrow, Kay."

"Bye, P. Have fun tonight." Karen winked at Persia before the two got into their cars. Karen started her car right up and pulled off in a rush. *Wonder why she's in such a hurry,* Persia thought.

"Call Le..." Persia attempted a command before she heard, *'Call from Jade.'*

"Hey, My Queen," Persia answered.

"Hey, My Qing. I want to cook for you tonight..." but before Jade could finish her statement, Persia cut her off.

"Awe, babe, I have plans tonight. I was just about to call you to let you know." Persia lied.

"What...what do you have planned for tonight?" Jade asked.

"I have plans with Lexi tonight. I have a late start in the morning, so I will see you in the morning, My Queen," Persia waited for Jade's response. The line was silent for 15 seconds, which felt like 15 minutes. "Jade?"

"Yes, Qing. Ok. I will see you in the morning. I love you." Jade gripped the back of a chair, her body starting to heat up with anger. She knew something wasn't right with Lexi when they spoke earlier.

"I love you too." Persia ended her call. She looked at herself in the rear-view mirror to unbutton the top couple of buttons on her shirt.

"Call Lexi." She commanded her car Bluetooth.

"Hey, Zaddi," Lexi cooed.

"Hey there, Gorgeous. How's your day?" Persia inquired.

"It was relaxing. I thought about you all day. It's been almost two weeks since I have had a chance to relax. You make sure that happens." Lexi thanked her.

"You a boss, baby; I have to make sure you take care of yourself too. What did you do today?" Persia asked.

"I went to the spa for the full package, facial, massage, hair removal, nails and toes, you know. I did a little shopping, and then I went to the grocery store. I spent the rest of the afternoon getting ready for you, Zaddi." Lexi answered.

"You were a busy woman. I'm on my way. I can't wait to see you." Persia started her car and pulled out of her parking space.

"See you soon, my love." Lexi hung up the phone and started lighting candles.

Chapter Three

"Yes, Qing. Ok. I will see you in the morning. I love you." Jade gripped the back of a chair, her body starting to heat up with anger. She knew something wasn't right with Lexi when they spoke earlier. She didn't hear anything Persia said before she hung up. Her mind kept running over her conversation with Lexi...she clearly lied about telling Persia she had plans. *I should just go over there and make it a threesome date.* Her leg rocked back and forth, rocking the chair; she hated feeling like this...feeling played.

"Fuck it if tonight is a date night, time to find me a date." Jade vengefully said to herself. Her voice echoed through their apartment. She picked up her phone and scrolled through her recent text messages. "Hmph. Let's see if Jayden is free tonight."

"Well, look who decided to grace my ears with her siren's song," Jayden answered.

"Hey, babe." Jade giggled. "Don't be an asshole."

"What other reason would you have to call me?" Jayden snapped back. He leaned back in his leather desk chair and propped his feet on his desk. He was intrigued by the call.

"Why would I call you? Obviously, you aren't interested in me." Jade responded.

"Now, Jade, are you fishing for where we stand?" Jayden split Jade's little act in two. He loved it when she tried her song on him. It kept things interesting between the two of them.

"No, I'm not. I'm telling the truth. A man calls a woman he is interested in." Jade held her breath for his response.

"You called me to tell me I'm not interested in you. This means wifey must be out for the night with one of her lovers. You're free tonight." Jayden read Jade. He waited a few seconds to give her a chance to deny it. She didn't. "Put on that short black dress that drops off your shoulder. I will send a car for you at 8. Stilettos, no stockings, and I will have your lingerie delivered within the hour."

"Cocktail or private date?" Jade knew better than to comment on any of Jayden's demands.

"It's just the two of us." He assured her.

"I will be ready at 8." Jade hung up the phone. She walked into her bedroom and fell on her bed with a huge smile. She was head over heels in love with Persia, but there was something about Jayden that sparked a different type of fire in her. It wasn't because he was a guy; it was the way he handled her. She didn't have to worry about anything. He made a lot of their decisions, including what Jade wore and where they went. She was rarely disappointed.

Less than an hour later, someone knocked at her door. She accepted the package Jayden had delivered. She was in love with the black lace piece; it would fit perfectly under her dress. He even included a new pair of red bottoms. Jade jumped up when she realized she had less than 2 hours left to get ready. Jayden's car was never late.

About 90 minutes later, Jade was sitting at her vanity, adding the finishing touches to her makeup. She wore his favorite perfume, the jewelry he bought her, and the dress and underwear she picked...she transformed herself from Persia's wifey to Jayden's concubine. Persia treated her very well, but Jayden spoiled her beyond anything she could have imagined. Her phone started vibrating.

"Hello, Ms. Peters. This is Jacob. I am downstairs," the driver alerted. Time had run out.

"Thank you, Jacob. I will be down in a few." Jade glanced at the clock. 8 o'clock on the dot. Good thing all she had left was her dress.

She slipped the black up her legs and covered the expensive piece of lace he called lingerie. She stared at her back in the mirror as she zipped herself up. *Why does it always have to be so hard*? She slid her feet into her new red bottoms that probably cost more than three months' rent. *Sometimes, it's just nice to feel like it's my life.* She wrapped her fur around her shoulders, picked up her clutch, and headed to the door. She turned around and scanned the apartment, and it felt like she was leaving a different version of herself behind. She slammed the front door as she exited and thought, *at least this version of me feels good.*

Chapter Four

"**G**ood evening, William." Persia greeted as the two started walking towards the elevator.

"How are you, Ms. Jefferson?" William inquired and pressed the up button on the elevator.

"I'm doing well, and yourself?" Persia asked.

"I am great. The night is beautiful. Have a good evening." William waved at Persia after she stepped onto the elevator.

"Have a great night, William," Persia responded. She could feel the anticipation building in her gut. She couldn't wait to see Lexi. Lexi was a breath of fresh air every time she saw her face. She stepped off the elevator and smelled the two dozen deep red long-stem roses she was holding behind her back. She knocked.

"I'm coming," Lexi yelled from inside her apartment. Persia could hear her scrambling before she opened the door. She swung the roses behind her back just as Lexi's beautiful chocolate smile peeked from behind the door.

"Hey there, Ms. Jefferson." Lexi smiled hard at the one hand behind Persia's back.

"Ms. Sims. May I come in?" Persia said formally.

"That is up to you." Lexi turned around and dropped her black silk robe to the floor, exposing the leather strap dress and hugging her curvaceous body. She started walking away from the door; the sound of her thigh-high black leather stiletto boots on the hardwood floors echoed throughout her apartment. Her six-inch boots raised her to 5 '7", almost eye to eye with Persia. "I have to finish getting dressed."

"You're not done?" Persia asked sarcastically. She picked up Lexi's rob, locked the front door, and scanned the living room. Lexi always went above and beyond when they saw each other. Persia could smell the steak, there were candles and flowers everywhere, and the music completed the romantic mood. Lexi made her second entrance after she finished getting dressed. Her dress was softly hugging her body as she glided into the living room.

"Wow!" Persia paused in awe of Lexi's beauty. The lace black mini dress was a soft change from the leather strap dress she had on moments before. Persia hoped that was a peak into their night together. She snapped out of her head and gave Lexi the roses.

"Thank you," Lexi hugged Persia. She went into the kitchen, put the roses in a vase, and poured two glasses of wine.

"You're welcome, it's my pleasure. You deserve much more," Persia said. Lexi blushed as she led Persia to the table. "What do we have here?"

"Dinner." Lexi directed Persia to sit and placed two plates on the table. "Your favorite." The two enjoyed the home-cooked meal while losing themselves in conversation. Every moment Persia spent with Lexi made life feel like light. She couldn't keep her hands off Lexi's sultry body. Dinner quickly turned into drinks on the couch.

"I'm going to change clothes, and you can relax at the table," Lexi pointed towards the massage table in the den.

"The black leather?" Persia was intrigued.

"Just go get comfortable." Lexi closed her bedroom door behind her. She reappeared with the black leather strap dress she had on earlier in the evening. This time, she had on thigh-high boots and a long ponytail to match.

"On the table!" Lexi demanded. Persia was already undressed down to her boxers and sports bra. A sly smile spread across Persia's face as she headed toward the massage table.

"Yes, ma'am," Persia responded. She laid across the table and let go. Lexi's hands roamed her body; every tense muscle, every knot was released.

"Turn," Lexi directed. Persia turned onto her back without opening her eyes. "Top off."

"No," Persia responded. She felt Lexi climb on top of her, straddling her. Persia came prepared and was already strapped up. She could feel Lexi grinding against her fake dick.

"Top off, now," Lexi directed again. Persia sat up and relinquished her sports bra. Only to meet Lexi for a kiss. Lexi quickly pulled away and stood up.

"On your knees!" Lexi picked up a short-riding whip and snapped it in the air. "Down."

"Yes, madam." Persia complied. Lexi snapped her whip in the air above Persia. She dropped a collection of leather and metal on the floor in front of Persia.

"Put it on," Lexi pushed the pile towards Persia. She complied again. Persia picked up the leather to find a fully strapped top. It resembled the sexy dress Lexi was wearing, except it had leather rings throughout. Persia got dressed. Lexi attached a leash to the ring just below Persia's neck.

"Back on the table." Lexi snapped her whip in the air, and it echoed through the apartment. She hurried onto the table and was strapped down to the massage table. Persia was moistening with anticipation as the whip grazed her stomach, with Lexi leering over her. It was an amazing night.

Chapter Five

"I enjoyed you, Jade," Jayden said. He lifted his body out of the bed, leaving Jade partially covered by the Egyptian cotton sheets. She lay on her stomach and looked up at him.

"I enjoyed our time, too," she responded. Jayden shot her a smile as he entered the bathroom. "Are you leaving?"

"Yes, I have an early morning. You can stay the night if you'd like," he told her. Jayden quickly showered and dressed. "Until next time," he kissed her on the forehead.

This feeling was too familiar for Jade. She knew Jayden had other plans for the night that pulled him away from her. She could never have him to herself. It saddened Jade to feel like Jayden could call on her whenever he wanted to pull her out to play. He didn't treat her like a toy, but sometimes she still felt like one.

Jade quickly got dressed after she heard the hotel room door close. She scanned the room for the rest of her things. She noticed a card on the table in front of the fireplace.

Jade,
Our time is always too short.
Which only makes me miss you more.
I hope this helps you fill some of the idle time.
Jayden

Tucked in the card sat six crisp one-hundred-dollar bills. Jade set the card back on the table and snapped a photo. Posted. She read the caption to herself.

WHAT I WOKE UP TO.
HE IS SO SWEET.

At least the rest of the world would see the beauty. She tucked the cash in her purse and left. Persia wouldn't be home tonight, so it's just her and her thoughts. A dangerous combination.

Chapter Six

"I love you," Lexi professed. She cuddled closer to Persia. She lay on her chest, listening to Persia's heart rate slow down.

"I love you too." Persia hugged her. The two quickly fell asleep, wrapped in each other. They woke the next morning with their bodies still locked into each other.

"Breakfast, my love?" Lexi asked. Persia agreed. She glanced at the clock. 7:45 a.m.

"I'm going to jump in the shower." Persia rubbed Lexi's face. "I don't want you to move."

"So, I will fix that." Lexi kissed Persia and got up. "Breakfast," she said, pointing at herself. "Shower," she pointed at Persia.

"DO YOU LIKE IT?" LEXI asked.

"Of course I do. Chocolate chip pancakes are my favorite. How about a little breakfast dessert?" Persia asked, pulling Lexi close to her.

Lexi wiped the syrup from her lip and smiled, "Now you know you don't have time."

"I'll always have time for you," Persia responded. Lexi melted in Persia's arms.

"I know, Zaddi," Lexi exhaled. She sat in Persia's lap, wrapped in her arms. "When will I see you again?"

"We will make plans soon. When are you free?" Persia asked.

"I have to go out of town in 2 days for a couple of weeks. Business. Can I see you before?" Lexi hoped.

"Damn. That's a long time. "Persia expressed. She scanned her calendar in her mind to see if she could make time for Lexi before she left. There's no way she'd make it that long. "Come by the office tomorrow for lunch."

Lexi lit up. "Okay." She kissed Persia again.

"I have to go. I told Jade I'd see her at home before I go to work," Persia stated. She could see the disappointment across Lexi's face. "But I will see you for lunch tomorrow."

"Yes, you will. Your turn to plan," Lexi smiled. She loved it when Persia set up their dates. She always had amazing surprises.

Persia collected her things, kissed Lexi, and rushed out the door.

Chapter Seven

When she entered her apartment, she instantly got annoyed. Jade swore she would be an amazing housewife, but Persia wondered how when she never cleaned up...even after herself. Her clothes from last night spanned from the front door to the bedroom. Shoe boxes, bras, underwear, dresses, etc. Persia skipped past it all. "Not today."

Jade was spread across their bed, still asleep...naked. Persia climbed into bed with her and woke her with kisses.

"Good morning," Jade responded.

"Did you miss me?" Persia inquired.

"Always. What time do you have to be at work?" Jade asked.

"Ten," Persia responded, looking at the clock. 8:45 a.m. She snuggled up behind Jade and inhaled her. Jade moaned with comfort.

"Did you have a date last night?" Persia asked.

"Yes. Jayden took me out," Jade said.

"You are regular with him now, huh?" Persia asked as she kissed Jade's neck.

"Yeah. He's good with everyone else. He doesn't want a lot, you know?" Persia knew exactly what Jade meant. Jade turned and started kissing Persia. "Lexi lied to me."

Persia's facial expression quickly changed from infatuation to annoyance. "Not this again," she responded.

"That's how you respond. Fuck it!" Jade turned back around.

"What did she lie about?" Persia knew she had to give Jade the benefit of at least hearing her out.

"She told me she had plans and wouldn't have time to see you last night," Jade whispered. She knew how Persia would respond. Jade had been the girl who cried wolf, always trying to make Lexi seem like a bad fit for their life.

"Really?" Persia already spoke to Lexi about what happened over dinner the night before. Jade turned to face Persia.

"I just wanted to do something for you yesterday. A surprise. I asked her if you all had plans. She said no, and I asked her to keep it that way so I could follow through with my surprise," Jade lied. She knew it wasn't the complete truth, but she doubted Lexi would tell Persia about what happened. Persia sat up and held Jade's hand.

"Lexi told me what happened. It didn't quite go like that, did it?" Persia asked. *She doesn't know Lexi has been recording their conversations for months.*

"So, you believe her?" Jade questioned. Persia seemed calm which always meant she was holding info back that she thought would be useful later.

"I'm asking you." Persia knew better than to get defensive.

"She didn't tell me you all had plans." Jade resorted to selective honesty.

"And you'll get an apology for that. She should have told you we had planned instead of playing on words," Persia responded. "I hadn't had a chance to tell you myself either, and I'm sorry."

"Thank you," Jade softened. She knew Persia wouldn't hear anything she had to say, but she had to try. "She didn't play on words. She lied. She can say it any way she wants, but... she is getting out of hand. How are we supposed to progress with that energy?"

My hope for a smooth conversation was crushed. There is no way Jade is going to let this go.

"I already cleared that up," Persia snapped. *There went our loving morning before work.* "Jade, if you have another issue with Lexi, you need to speak on that. Speak up and be honest."

"I don't want you dating Lexi anymore. We are going to get married one day, and she isn't invited!" Jade stood up. Persia sat up and put her head in her hands. "And you lied to me."

Here we go again.

"Look, Persia. I know this life was good for us dating, but we live together. I want to spend my life with you." Jade said. Persia didn't respond. "I don't want her in this with us."

"I told you when we got together... I am poly. You said you were good with that," Persia responded.

"Who doesn't like to play a little, but you are taking this too far? I want exclusivity," Jade stated. Persia threw her hands in the air and walked out of the room. Jade followed. "Are you listening? Am I even worth it?"

"It's not about that Jade. I knew this would happen. My poly life isn't something that happens when I'm dating or single. I want to build a life with more than one partner. I hope you will be a part of it. I'm not monogamous... at all," Persia explained.

"Not even for me? I'm not worth that?" Jade asked again.

"Look..." Persia softly grabbed Jade by her shoulders and spoke unbelievably softly. "...my poly life is not a result of my feelings for you. It's the way I choose to live my life."

"So that's my answer. I'm not enough for you," Jade cried.

"What? No. Listen to me. Stop thinking you are the answer to every person's dream woman. Shit. Maybe we wouldn't be here. You would have heard me when I told you who I am." Persia was visibly annoyed at having the same argument. *Jade didn't understand. She acts as if the way I'm living is wrong. I was truly clear about what I wanted. I even explained how I wanted my household to work. I changed a lot but was okay with it for Jade. She wanted our life to be separate from our lovers, so we lived together, just the two of us. I wasn't comfortable with the idea, but I love her.* Persia was lost in her own thoughts.

"What are you trying to say?" Jade asked. Persia could see tears building in her eyes.

"You knew who I was when we got together. This isn't about Lexi. It's about you and me," Persia paused. *I love Jade. Do I want to try monogamy? This is crazy.*

"It's about you not wanting me... or just me. There's something wrong with you, Persia. How can you be okay with another person touching all over me? You're okay with me possibly falling in love with someone else?" Jade was finally being honest.

"Yes, I am," Persia responded. Jade let her tears flow.

"You're going to be late for work," Jade stated through her tears. They both glanced at the clock. 9:27 a.m.

"I love you, Jade. I am in love with you. I love our life together. I want us to continue to grow together." Persia responded.

"I know," Jade answered. "Just not enough to only want me." She walked into her office and closed the door. Persia could hear the door lock. She wouldn't see Jade before she left. She attempted to say goodbye, but Jade's music canceled any outside noise... including her knocks.

Chapter Eight

"Oh no, Lexi, you are always welcome. Especially when you bring food." Karen and Lexi walked into Persia's office.

"Karen, why are you back in here?" Persia took a shot at Karen before hugging and kissing Lexi.

"Hey, Zaddi," Lexi greeted Persia, then turned to hand Karen a plate.

"To get my food," Karen smirked.

"How do you get food for my lunch date?" Persia turned to glare at Lexi, "And I'm supposed to be taking you out."

"You are, but I know she loves my cooking," Lexi responded softly.

"Keep playing, and we both will end up with her," Karen pointed at Lexi while playfully threatening Persia. Karen sat down and opened the white container. "Just like the restaurant."

"Where to today?" Lexi laughed at Karen and then turned her attention to Persia.

"You'll see, babe," Persia responded. "K, get out."

"Oh, it's like that now she's here," Karen pointed at Lexi playing insulted. "Ok, ok. I'll go, but I'm taking your snack with me." Karen snatched another container out of the bag and then left the office. Both Persia and Lexi laughed.

"Are you ready?" Lexi was excited about their date.

Persia led Lexi to her car while sharing the morning's events. Lexi was visibly disgusted when Persia assured her she'd have to apologize for playing with Jade. She rarely put up a fight when she was given directions; this time was no different. *I can't keep going forward if we can't get these things under control. I love Jade too much.*

"You are working really hard to keep this MONOGAMOUS woman in our POLYAMOROUS relationship." Lexi emphasized the relationship types, hoping Persia would catch her drift. They rode most of the ride silently; Persia didn't know how to respond.

I know Lexi doesn't understand what Jade and I have, but she doesn't see Jade like I do. She can't see what I see when it's just the two of us. She shared a part of her that was off-limits to everyone else.

"Baby, you know it's not my style to be all in your relationships. I will not let you set yourself up to get hurt again by this woman," Lexi continued.

Lexi was never fully on board with Jade after she almost messed things up in the beginning. Jade was completely okay with multiple lovers but had an issue with Lexi. Instead of talking about it with the two of us, Jade decided to get back at me for how I made her feel. I had no idea she was even bothered because she never said anything to me. She slept with a close friend of mine and lied about it. They played me by being in my face as if we were all friends, but the entire time, they sneaked off together behind my back. The deception was harmful, but we were able to get past it. Lexi never did.

"I wish she would have been honest with me," Persia said.

"She was…at the time. Things change, baby. She fell in love with you," Lexi tried to help as much as she could, but she knew Jade wouldn't last. She was too insecure for this life. Not to mention, she believed in monogamy. "She wants you to only want her."

The car came to a stop. They were at the aquarium. Lexi's favorite.

"We're having lunch here?" Lexi was practically jumping in her seat.

"Lunch and more," Persia answered.

The two entered the aquarium; it was much quieter than usual. Persia led Lexi toward the dolphins. Lexi started smiling as soon as she saw the table for two in front of the dolphin's pool.

"Ladies, may I escort you to your table?" an older gentleman appeared. He led them to the table, where Persia pulled Lexi's chair out. Candles were lit, the table was set perfectly, and the food smelled delicious. "The show will start momentarily. May I bring you something to drink?"

"We will both have a tequila sunrise," Persia ordered. The gentleman nodded, then walked away. He quickly returned with their drinks and salads.

Persia held Lexi's hand, "I want to focus on you right now." Lexi rubbed Persia's hand, then retracted her own.

"Baby, you and Jade are a part of me too. If you aren't good, it will spill over into your other relationships." Lexi was right. Persia had to find a solution for her and Jade.

"I know. Every time we speak about it, all she hears is I want someone else. The little rivalry between you two isn't helping.

"Persia, baby, it doesn't matter what goes on between her and me. She came into this with the intention of getting you to herself." Lexi corrected. "But... I can acknowledge how our interactions can gas up the situation."

"Thank you. I will have a talk with her when I get home tonight," Persia said reluctantly.

"Good. Now, back to us," Lexi smiled.

"You still have to apologize," Persia reiterated.

"Fine!" Lexi agreed. The older gentleman returned with their main course. Lexi was confused because they didn't order, but Persia assured her their orders were given before they arrived. They were finishing up their lunch when the music started playing.

"Alexis and Persia, please turn your attention to the pool. Someone wants to greet you!" a voice announced in surround sound.

A dolphin flew out of the water and flipped. It turned trick after trick, entertaining the couple with its personality and skill. The dolphin swam to the edge of the pool near the two, pointing at a bucket of fish.

"I want to feed her," Lexi said, jumping up and heading towards the bucket.

"Ma'am, please, let us handle the feeding," a young woman in a scuba suit yelled, running towards Lexi. Lexi stepped back with disappointment. "I'm sorry. Hi. I'm Jenna. The trainer."

Lexi shook her hand. Persia sat back, watching her lover in excitement. The trainer held Lexi's hand as she explained how to feed the dolphin. Persia could tell the trainer was flirting. Bold. Lexi is an attractive, confident woman; people are always drawn to her. Her plus size, curvaceous body, milk chocolate skin, deep eyes, and vibrant smile were like bait in a sea of piranhas. It turned Persia on to see Lexi with someone else.

"Did you see me? I love dolphins. She let me touch her," Lexi reported with excitement.

"I saw you. You are much braver than I am," Persia responded. Lexi jumped in her lap, picking off her plate and ignoring her full plate only a few inches away.

"Thank you for today. This was my first time touching a dolphin," Lexi smiled.

"There it is. That's all I need right there." Persia pointed to Lexi's smile.

"I love you," Lexi kissed Persia. "Time to go."

They returned to Persia's job. Karen was still in the lunchroom. After a quick goodbye, Persia walked Lexi to her car and then returned to join Karen.

"Have fun?" Karen sarcastically asked.

"Shut up... yeah. I took her to a private lunch at the aquarium. Touching dolphins. Private show. She loved it." Persia glowed while talking about Lexi. "It's so easy and honest with her."

"Damn, bro, you said that *easy and honest* with some weight to it. Are you good?" Karen was concerned.

Yeah, it's just Jade. She's giving me a hard time." Persia put her head in her hand.

"That looks like more than just a hard time. Let it out," Karen pushed.

"She wants monogamy," Persia said.

"Oh, dayum. What are you going to do?" As long as they've known each other, Persia has practiced polyamory. Karen knew this day would come, but Persia just didn't want to listen. Jade has always shown signs of disdain for Persia's lovers... Lexi, in particular. She just couldn't ask for it to stop because she didn't want to give up her own. She wanted Persia to be committed only to her.

"I don't know K. I really don't know," Persia stated.

"You know how Jade is. Right? Don't you deserve to be with someone that values you? That can offer as much as they ask for. The only consistent thing about Jade is her constant hypocrisy." Karen grabbed her friend's hand. "What's keeping you with her?"

"Come on now, Karen. Damn," Persia responded.

"Are you going to answer?" Karen waited.

"I think... I just can't be without her. I love her... I'm addicted to her. She's really like a drug to me. It's good while we are in it." Persia answered.

"I love you, P. And I will support whatever you decide. But you really need to take a clear look at your situation. Even in her polyamory, she still can't be honest with you. Am I wrong? Did she ever really explain what happened... you know... with the accident," Karen asked. "We know she messed with ole girl, but you all were good when the accident happened. You just let things go with her." She knew Persia didn't want to hear or talk about that incident, but it was relevant.

"Shit. She never explains anything fully. She gave some vague story to make it seem like she was with her brother, but we both know she was with ole girl even after she told me they were done." Persia couldn't give a valid reason for staying with Jade other than the love... the addiction. "I thought we were getting better."

"Persia, you know I love you, and you are my bro for life." She didn't want to continue out of fear... fear of Persia's response. "She's never going to respect you. You've given her too many chances."

Persia didn't respond. She just sat staring at Karen. What was she supposed to say? Everyone around her was telling her to leave it alone, but her heart didn't know how to let go.

Chapter Nine

"I love you, Jade. I am in love with you. I love our life together. I want us to continue to grow together." Persia responded.

"I know," Jade answered. "Just not enough to only want me." She walked into her office and closed the door. She slowly locked the door behind her. She knew Persia would try to come to see her before she left for work, and she just couldn't take it. Jade pulled out her Bluetooth speaker and started playing her favorite playlist.

Jade ran a small marketing firm. It was enough to allow her to live comfortably. She sat at her desk, staring at the black screen of her laptop as the lyrics and bass roamed through her body.

"Ugh. I need to snap out of it," she said to herself. She quickly opened her computer and pulled up Alex's page.

Alex and Jade met a while back before she met Persia. Jade always had a little bit of a thing for Alex but didn't think Alex was interested in her. After Persia and Jade got together, she realized they all knew each other but didn't tell Persia. At the time, she didn't know why, but it quickly unfolded. Alex and Persia became acquainted quickly but only as a tool for Alex to get closer to Jade. Alex shows her intentions to Jade at a party when she kisses Jade on the dance floor. It shocked Jade, but it also intrigued her. Alex knew that after Jade didn't tell her lover about the advances, she had a chance. Jade and Alex began a secret affair that lasted months. They lied and hid everything from Persia and Alex's girlfriend. When Persia found out, it almost crushed their relationship, but Jade vowed never to go there with Alex again and to maintain their rules, which included not dating mutual friends. Shortly after, Alex proposed to her girlfriend. Alex and Jade didn't talk much after that.

"Until now..." Jade whispered to herself, scrolling through Alex's page. She clicked the messenger button and paused. "Am I really ready to do this..." She sent one word...hey.

DING Jade's phone buzzed on the desk next to her. It was a text message from Alex. '*Can we talk?*'

She texted back quickly before she lost her nerve. She told Alex to give her a call, and her phone rang. "Hello?"

"Hey there, Jade," Alex responded. Jade didn't know how to react or if she should be on the phone with Alex at all. She knew their situationship would only get worse with regular conversations. "Are you there?"

"Hey Alex, sorry my Bluetooth was disconnected," she lied. "How are you, stranger? I haven't heard from you in a while."

"I'm not doing good. I am, but my head is messed up. You have always been the one that helped me clear my head. Can I talk to you about Kyla?" Alex asked.

"Oh wow. Of course, Alex. What's wrong?" Jade leaned back in her office chair and ran her fingers across her bare skin. She listened to Alex vent about her fiancée and how their relationship was falling apart. Alex was attempting to be a better spouse, but it seemed to be too late for her fiancée. She was tired and uninterested in Alex. Jade gave her genuine advice; she knew nothing compared to loving someone who didn't love you back the same way you loved them. They sat and talked for hours. Alex made Jade feel like someone was listening again; someone really cared about what she felt and said.

"Thank you for talking to me, Jade. It's so easy to talk to you. I wish it were this easy with her," Alex confessed. "I just want to be more to her than her benefactor. But how can I be upset at her for looking at me that way when I've never acted like she was worth anything more to me."

"Look, Alex, it's not over if you don't want it to be. You will have to put in some real work." Jade wanted black love to win, and she cared about Alex and her fiancée. "I will help you."

"Thank you, Jade, really, thank you. It feels amazing just to have someone listen." Alex said.

"My pleasure, you're my friend. I'm here for you." Jade responded. They wrapped up their conversation. Alex promised to take Jade out to thank her, and Jade agreed.

All I need now is...Jayden.

Jade studied herself in the mirror. She had to decide if she was going to call Jayden to fully get out of her head or *FUCK THIS BITCH UP*. It's on Lexi that Persia was thinking like this. Persia won't be honest about her thoughts, but Jade saw it from her actions. She was different. Jade wasn't going to let Persia play her as dumb. The phone rang again.

"Jade, I need to see you," Jayden stated.

"I was just thinking of you," Jade responded.

"What's wrong?" Jayden inquired.

"Lexi...Persia...this whole multiple lovers thing. It's getting sticky," Jade replied.

"Leave her and come be mine," Jayden offered frequently.

"You don't want JUST me either," Jade cut him off.

"You would be the center of my house and heart. Lovers wouldn't come before you. I'm not here to convince you. I have more important matters." Jayden got quiet.

"I know it's just..." Jade started.

"Be ready in an hour. Go to the door and get your dress. My driver will be outside soon," Jayden directed, and the line went quiet.

"Jayden?" Jade checked to see if Jayden was still on the line. No response. Jade instantly sent Persia a text letting her know about her plans with Jayden for the night. *I shouldn't have texted her.*

Jade began getting dressed with Alex on her mind. The phone rang, and she answered quickly.

"Ms. Peters, I am ready for you." The driver quickly spoke before Jade could say hello.

"Thank you. I will be down shortly," Jade responded.

The red dress from Jayden swept against the ground and draped low on her back. The neckline was conservative, but the split was telling it all. He matched shoes and jewelry perfectly. Before she could get into the car, Jayden texted her.

Join me for my company's holiday gala.

As soon as the town car's door opened, the camera flashes blinded Jade. A familiar hand reached into the car and helped her onto the red carpet. Jayden smiled as he took in her beauty.

"Tonight is going to be an amazing night," he smiled at Jade. They walked the red carpet together and then made a grand entrance into the ballroom. There were quite a few whispers and surprised faces. "This is my first time attending one of our holiday galas."

"Really," Jade laughed. "How many years has the company thrown galas?"

"This is our fifth year. I always thought my employees wouldn't want to let loose if the big boss was here. Tonight, we will see." Jade said. An intoxicated Asian man stumbled towards Jayden, pointing at him.

"Wooooo! He's actually here," he slurred. "He came. You came. I can't believe you actually showed up this year."

Jade stood back with caution, but Jayden calmed her concern. "Wick, you having a good time?"

"Yeah, Jay. It's going great. Thanks for having it at a hotel this year. Me and the wife got a room upstairs. It's going to be a great party," Wick slurred.

"Let's go get a drink," Jayden asked. Jade gave him a look that expressed her disdain for this man getting any drunker, but he waved her off. He knew what he was doing. The waitress returned with five drinks. The guys took a shot each, then grabbed a second glass that turned out to be water. Jayden handed Jade a glass of champagne. "Always know, I know what I'm doing. The shot was a watered-down shot of vodka; he didn't know the difference."

"My apologies for ever doubting you," Jade said playfully.

"Would you like to dance?" Jayden asked. Jade agreed by taking his hand. They danced all night. Jayden finally got his chance to enjoy time with his employees outside of the office. It was a party to remember.

The evening was slowing to an end. Jayden and Jade enjoyed their last dance, "Are you ready to leave, beautiful Jade?"

"Yes, I am, sir," Jade replied. They walked towards the table, and a vibration came from her clutch. She checked her phone to see who was calling but didn't answer.

"Is everything okay?" Jayden was concerned.

"Yes, just a girl thing. I'm going to call her back. Give me a second?" Jade requested. Jayden agreed; he needed to go say his goodbyes. Jade slipped into the hallway and called Alex back.

"What's wrong?" Jade whispered.

"Nothing could be wrong if I'm talking to you," Alex replied.

"Alex, I can't talk right now. Is everything okay?" Jade asked.

"Yes, everything is fine. You're busy?" Alex inquired.

"Yes, I am, but I will call you tomorrow?" Jade needed to get off the phone soon. Jayden hated when she spoke to others when they were with each other. Their time was so sparse already.

"Too busy for me?" Alex asked, but her tone concerned Jade. She sounded like she was hanging on the answer.

"I am never too busy for you, Alex. Right now, I am in the middle of something, and I will give you a call in the morning to check on you, ok." Jade stated this time, not giving another option.

"Jade?" Jayden grabbed her arm, startling her.

"I am ready," Jade dropped her phone to her side to kiss Jayden. He was aware of what Jade was doing but decided to give her a few minutes to finish up.

"I will be right back; I have one more." Jayden pointed into the crowd and then walked off.

"Alex, are you there?" Jade put the phone back to her ear.

"Are you out with someone else?" Alex said with a raised voice.

"Good night, Alex," Jade stated, then disconnected the call.

She met Jayden outside, waiting for their driver. "Mmmm, I can't wait to get back to your place."

"I have a surprise for you," Jayden smiled. He helped her into the town car. Jade was intoxicated but still alert to what was going on. She pulled her red dress up to her hips, then straddled Jayden.

"I want you right now." Jade started unbuttoning Jayden's pants while kissing him. Jayden picked her up off of him and sat her back in the seat. He buttoned his pants and then pulled her dress back down.

"I have a surprise for you. We are almost there. Put this on." He handed her a blindfold. She complied.

Once they reached his home, he guided her through the house and into his bedroom. He sat her on the bed and disappeared.

"Jayden?" she said. "Are you there?"

"Stand up." He commanded. She complied. He undressed her. "Sit down."

She began to feel hands rubbing all over her body. The soft kisses. Jade tried to lean back to enjoy the attention, but a hand stopped her. The kisses were all over her body.

"Who are you? I know you aren't Jayden." Jade questioned.

"Don't ask questions," the mystery woman said between kisses. She continued to indulge in Jade's body.

"STOP! I don't know you!" Jade felt uncomfortable and no longer wanted to continue.

"Calm Jade. I am here. You're safe." Jayden assured her. The kisses started again, but this time, there were more lips, more hands, and more tongues.

His hands and mouth, in addition to the mystery woman's tongue between her legs, sent her into ecstasy. When she could move again, Jade attempted to take off her blindfold, but she stopped her.

"No, he doesn't want it off. Obey," she demanded.

"What's your name?" Jade asked quietly.

"Don't talk. We aren't allowed. Stop worrying and relax. I am here for you," she responded.

"Oh. My. God." Jade moaned. Four hands. Two sets of lips. Two tongues. Jade flipped into another intense orgasm.

"That's good. Step back," Jayden commanded. Jade didn't feel the woman's body anymore. "Was she good, sweetness?"

"She was...is delicious," the mystery woman licked her lips.

"Take off your blindfold," Jade obeyed his request. He stood in front of her naked, and a beautiful chocolate woman was kneeling beside her. Her hair was pulled tight into a bun. Her body was succulent, but she only stared at the floor. There was a collar around her neck.

"What do you think?" Jayden asked.

"She was better than you," Jade said confusingly, looking at his flaccid dick.

"She should be; pleasure is her specialty," he responded. The comparison would never bother him, and Jade knew that.

"What's wrong with her?" Jade felt weird with her kneeling quietly.

"Nothing. She's my submissive. Greet Jade." Jayden directed the woman.

"Nice to finally meet you, Jade. He's told me so much about you," she said, then quickly rose and hugged Jade. "I'm Cashmere."

"Nice to meet...and experience you, Cashmere." Jade looked at Jayden. "I hope to see you more?"

"Absolutely. If you want more Cashmere, then you shall have her. Right?" Jayden looked at Cashmere for an answer.

"Whatever my King and Queen want," she replied. Cashmere looked at Jayden for his permission to continue to interact with Jade. He nodded. She embraced Jade as if she'd been waiting forever. They kissed while wrapped in each other. Jade could still taste herself on her soft lips.

"I love him. I am his..." Cashmere whispered in Jade's ear. "...if you join us. I will be yours also. Think about it."

Cashmere kissed Jayden, "Good night, you two."

"Where are you going? Where is she going? I want her to stay," Jade turned to Jayden.

"She doesn't sleep with us unless invited. She has her own bedroom." He pulled Jade in closer. "I didn't want to overwhelm either of you, first time meeting."

"You're right," she agreed. "Especially since I want my time with you."

Jayden picked up Jade into his arms. She wrapped her legs around his waist. "I feel dirty; I believe we need a shower," he said.

A smile spread across Jade's face. He carried her to the bathroom. Their romantic bath was just the beginning of their evening together. It turned Jade on more, knowing Cashmere was still in the house.

Chapter Ten

A month passed quickly since Jade met Cashmere, and Alex became a regular in her life. Things seem to get better for Persia and Jade. They didn't argue as much, and Jade didn't complain about Lexi anymore. Jade spent more time out than usual, but Persia didn't see anything wrong with it.

Persia lay with Jade on her chest, watching her as she slept. She ran her fingers through Jade's hair. *Time has made us better.* Jade's phone vibrated on the nightstand. It was Alex. *What the hell is she doing on Jade's phone?*

"Hey, Alex," Persia answered, showing no concern in her voice.

"Oh…Persia. Hey. Uh, is Jade around?" Alex said with uncertainty.

"She's right here asleep. I'll tell her to call you when she wakes up?" Persia wondered how often they spoke. *They aren't supposed to speak at all. Alex sounded suspicious.* Persia scanned the call history; something wasn't right. They rarely spoke during the day but frequently had long conversations in the middle of the night…*after I am asleep. Damn, even the nights we had sex. She still got out of our bed to spend hours on the phone with her. Every night for a month, and never said anything to me.*

Persia set the phone back on the nightstand and hugged Jade. *Even when she can date whomever she'd like, she still insists on lying about it. She doesn't trust me.*

"Mmmm. Hey, good morning, My Qing," Jade stretched into hugging Persia.

"Good morning, My Queen. Alex called; she said to call her back when you wake up." Persia waited for a response. Nothing.

"Ok, Qing, but first, I want to spend some time with you." She kissed Persia's face all over. The two cuddled for a couple of hours before Persia had to get up. It was a Saturday morning, but Persia still had things to do.

"Time for me to head out. First..." Persia grabbed Jade's face softly and stared into her eyes. "...are we doing better and being completely honest with each other?"

"Yes, Qing. Things are much better now." Jade smiled genuinely. Persia searched her face for the truth, but she didn't let it peak through. Lexi and Persia also spent more time together over the last month. Persia wasn't worried about Alex; she was concerned about the deception.

"I love you, Jade, baby." Persia jumped up to kiss all over Jade's body. They began wrestling playfully. Persia decided to let the Alex situation go. Maybe she can help Jade trust her again.

BOOM BOOM BOOM

"I got it, baby; I'll be right back!" Jade ran to the front door. Persia jumped up naked and grabbed her clothes. She couldn't get dressed fast enough. All she could hear was a bunch of whispering that made her pause in her steps.

"You can't be here," she heard someone whisper.

"What the hell is going on?" Persia interrupted.

"We need to talk!" Jade said.

"No need to talk. This is what it is. Jade is coming with me. She doesn't want the crazy ass life you are living. She just wants one person who loves her. That's me." Alex yelled while pushing Jade behind her.

Persia laughed, "Is that right?" She looked at Jade, "You're back at this, huh?"

"It is. I'm tired of my Queen shacking up with you! You couldn't take care of her, so I will." Alex stood strong in her statement.

Persia paused. Then began laughing, "There you go." Persia pushed Jade towards Alex. "Take her. I assume you all have been with each other again, and I'm not talking about friends."

"Persia, Qing, it's not what it looks like," Jade tried to grab Persia, but her hands were pushed away. "Listen."

"Alex, bro, she didn't tell you she is in this voluntarily? She has lovers...apparently more than me." Persia smiled. "Jade?"

"Stop trying to make this about her. You don't know how to take care of a woman," Alex said angrily. Persia laid her hand out towards Jade. Both Alex and Persia were now looking at Jade. She didn't say anything.

"Jade!" Alex yelled. Jade was startled but still didn't talk.

"Let me help because we have been here before, haven't we?" Persia asked Jade, but she refused to answer. "Right Alex? You're not the only lover Jade wasn't honest with. I can't be mad at you; I would do the same thing if she sold me the story; she sold you. I'm her only lover, right? But she picked you up, too, right? But she's not poly? Jayden is her male lover, but he only wants her when he calls. She has me...but of course, I don't love her. All I want is other women. Then there's the fem. What's her name, Jade? I can never remember, especially since she only wants her when she calls her. Then there's you. Her special big secret because she is a victim in this."

Persia could see the anger and hurt across Alex's face. Jade's face went stone cold by this time.

"And what about Kyla, Alex? Did you end that?" Persia asked.

"Don't talk about Kyla," Alex snapped. "Is this true?"

"Alex, I told you I wasn't trying to leave anyone for you. I enjoy our time, but hell, I was helping you with your fiancée just a couple of weeks ago. Now you're at my door trying to break up my relationship. Damn, Alex. Why couldn't we just keep what we had? Where is Kyla?" Jade snapped.

"What!?!" Alex was flabbergasted. She took a step back and looked at Persia, then Jade. "Is this some crazy shit you all do?"

"Whoa, Alex, slow your roll. Remember, this had nothing to do with me. You came here." Persia laughed. "Now, my patience is quickly running low. Jade, go get your bag. Your great love has come to rescue you."

"Persia, stop it. I'm not going anywhere. We will work this out. Alex, I think it's time for you to leave." Jade attempted to guide Alex to the door, but she wasn't going anywhere. "Please, Alex."

"We will work nothing out. Grab your go bag, and you can all come pick up the rest later. I hope Kyla is ready to have a sister wife." Persia laughed.

"Shut the fuck up about Kyla!" Alex lunged at Persia.

"Alex, No!" Jade jumped between Alex and Persia. Persia didn't move. She stared at the situation in slow motion as if she wasn't a part of it, but she had no fear.

"Fuck this. I will show you." Alex said as she rushed past Persia and Jade, heading for their bedroom. Persia and Jade followed. Alex pulled the bottom drawer out of Jade's dresser and let it land on the floor. She pulled the clothes out of the drawer for effect.

"Jade, what the fuck is that?" Persia stated.

Jade's face went blank, and she was silent again. Alex went for their bookshelf. She opened a tin canister Jade used to hold her memories. Alex poured the tin on the floor, and out came a rainstorm of letters. She didn't stop there. She headed towards Jade's shelf on the wall.

"Alex, stop!" Jade yelled while pulling at Alex.

"Just stop!" Alex jerked away and grabbed three photos that were lying flat on the shelf. She threw those in the pile on the floor.

"What is all this, Alex?" Persia calmly asked. She knew this was the time for her to get the truth. It was ready to come to light.

"These are Jade's favorite pictures of her and me after all these years. She keeps them on her shelf. She just can't stand them up, or you would know what they were." Alex pointed to the pile of letters on the floor. "These are all the letters I wrote her. Every single one. All these years, and she kept them all." Persia looked at Jade; *who are you?* "Wait, I'm not done." Alex picked up the drawer off the floor.

"Is that a fucking dildo?" Persia was stunned. She didn't keep her toys in the drawers. She had a special box for all of that. So, this was something Jade was trying to hide. By this time, Jade was sitting on their bed with her head in her hands.

"This is my dick, special for Jade. We picked it out together, and she said she would keep it to make sure no one else was getting used to it." Alex emptied the bag that held the dildo and other items. "Those are my condoms, lube, butt plug...oh, and those are the clothes I forgot the last time I spent the night."

"Here?" Persia stared at Jade while talking to Alex. "Are you done?"

"Yes, here. I'm almost done." Alex stood in front of Jade while she sat on the bed. "Get up, darling."

"No, you're done, Alex," Jade begged with her eyes.

"Not yet, I'm not." Alex picked Jade up and placed her in a chair. Then she flipped over their mattress. Alex and Persia both looked at the restraints that Persia knew nothing about that were tucked under their mattress. "Now, I'm done."

"THEN GET THE FUCK OUT!" Jade screamed. Persia grabbed a duffel bag and began stuffing Jade's clothes in it. "What are you doing?"

"Jade, it's time to go," Persia stated with no emotion at all.

"Persia, we can talk about this after Alex leaves." Jade turned to Alex, "You've exposed me, now can you leave?"

"It's time for you both to leave," Persia said. She took the full duffel bag into the living room and sat it at the front door. Jade and Alex followed her. "Don't forget your stuff, Alex." Persia grabbed another duffel out of the coat closet and headed back toward their bedroom.

"Jade, how can you do this? We were building something." Alex asked. "All I want you to do is be honest so we can be together."

"Alex, I don't want to be with you. We had fun together, and you made me feel special. We are friends and lovers, but it's time to let the lovers part go," Jade confessed.

"I was going to leave Kyla for you...for us," Alex replied, confused.

"You came here for me. You haven't told Kyla yet? Alex, go home to your fiancée. Don't call me for a while. We need some time to let this go," Jade said. Persia returned to the living room with the full duffel bag; she tossed it at Alex's feet.

"Is there anything else in here that belongs to you, Alex?" Persia asked.

"Naw. Nothing here belongs to me." Alex stared at Jade. She picked up the duffel and walked out the front door.

Persia turned to Jade, "Your turn."

"My Qing, just talk to me. We can work this out. I love you." Jade requested.

"This isn't the type of love I'm interested in. We're done, Jade. You can keep the phone; you have until the end of this month to put it in your name. You can set up a time to come get the rest of your stuff. Furniture and such, you'll need a U-Haul." Persia said. Jade just stared at the emptiness in her former lover's eyes.

"Persia?" Jade started.

"Look, Jade, I need some time. Just give me at least that." Persia stated.

Jade knew there was nothing else she could say. She picked up her duffel bag and put on her slides before walking out the front door. Persia allowed her body to relax on the couch. Tears started flowing down her face.

Chapter Eleven

"P, bro, I haven't seen you in almost a week." Karen rushed into Persia's office. *I needed the time to get my head right.*

"A lot has happened, so I took some personal time." Persia leaned back in her chair. Karen sat down.

"Well, let it out," Karen responded. Persia spilled everything that happened. Karen sat with her mouth open.

"She really had Alex lingering all in your house like that. What are you going to do?" Alex asked. "Where did Jade go?"

"Yeah. I'm not sure where she is, but she is probably with Jayden. This whole thing is because she wanted monogamy." Persia said.

"Bro, this woman...she is not the one for you. I don't know if she knows what she wants," Karen responded. "You are going to go monogamous for her, aren't you?"

"I think it's the least I can do." Persia looked away.

"What about Lexi? You can't drop Lexi," Karen begged.

"I'm going to have to. This whole thing is crazy, but the reason Jade acts so crazy all over the place is because she wants someone to love her unconditionally. Show her she is worth it. I think." Persia went on, "Lexi and I haven't seen much of each other over the last month or so anyway. She has a lot going on with her job and family. She goes through these spurts where she doesn't have a lot of time. This worked so well because of that," Persia responded. Karen leaned back in her chair with her hand on her chin.

"Then you need to find Jade and tell her," Karen said. "And you both can drop everyone else."

"Bro! I really don't want to drop Lexi." Persia slapped her forehead. "Damn."

"Man, you don't know what you want." Karen laughed. "Figure that shit out before you do anything. Can you even trust Jade anymore after everything Alex showed you in your own home? After she did this again with the same person?"

"To be honest, I don't know K. I'm willing to try and work through it with her. It was really fucked up, but with us being polyamorous, it probably doesn't hit me the same way as it would you. You know?" Persia responded.

"Naw, bro, I don't know. I'm not talking about having sex with someone else in your home. That's nothing; you have all done that before. I'm talking about the home you pay for and relax in as your sanctuary. She defiled that by bringing someone else into your home and allowing them to relax that much." Karen stated. Karen's anger was all over her face.

"Come on, K, you know I don't look at property like that. If I did, I would have a problem with anything Lexi does in her apartment when I'm not there. I'm taking care of everything there, too." Persia responded. Karen nodded. "She messed me up by getting involved with someone and lying to them and me. I will have a hard time getting past the deception again."

"True, ok." Karen changed her expression. It slipped her mind that Persia took care of multiple apartments for her lovers. "So, you know what you want to do?"

"I'm going to do this for Jade, but I'm going to miss the hell out of Lexi. Damn." Persia shook her head.

"You texted her, didn't you?" Karen leaned in.

"Who?" Persia had a fake, confused look.

"You know damn well who, Lexi. Did you text her?" Karen asked.

"Ummm..." Persia saw the 'don't bullshit me' look on Karen's face. *I tell her everything else anyway.* "...I did."

"I'm done. Y'all going out?" Karen started pacing.

"I told her I wanted to come see her tonight, nothing formal. just a night together." Persia responded.

"Oh, so this is supposed to be your last night together?" Karen wasn't feeling it.

"She won't know it. I don't know what's going to happen when I go talk to Jade." Persia hung her head.

"Just don't tell her. Have an amazing night, and don't mess it up talking about this shit. Your word?" Karen leaned on her desk towards Persia.

"My word, bro," Persia promised. "Now get the hell out of here and go do some work."

"I'm working even when I'm not," Karen chuckled. "I'll see you for lunch?"

"Yeah, close my door on your way out," Persia agreed. Karen nodded as she headed out of Persia's office. A text notification from Lexi vibrated Persia's phone.

Change in plans. Meet me at the Four Seasons Room 648.

PERSIA'S INTEREST WAS piqued. She wasn't used to her lovers sending her texts like this; it was even better for our last night together.

Persia finished her day smoothly. After work, she swung by her apartment and grabbed an overnight bag. She decided to call Lexi on the way to the hotel.

"Hey, I'm just calling to let you know I'm on my way," Persia said.

"I miss you. See you soon." Lexi hung up.

The directions said Persia was about 4 minutes away from the hotel when her phone rang.

"Hello?" She answered.

"Hey, can we talk?" It was Jade. Persia paused. "Are you there?"

"Yeah, I'm here. What do we need to talk about?" Persia asked.

"I don't want it to end the way it did. We need to have some closure. We need to talk. I'm available in 20 minutes at the park. You know which one." Jade stated. She held her breath on the other end, waiting for Persia's response.

"Ok. I will be there in 15 minutes, but I can't stay long." Persia responded. She'd have to be late to see Lexi; there was a chance that she wouldn't see her at all tonight. Persia's heart dropped into the seat. She passed the hotel and headed for the park. She called Lexi to let her know she had to make an emergency stop and would be about 30-45 minutes late. Lexi was sad but agreed.

When Persia pulled into the park's parking lot, she saw Jade was already there. Persia's heart was beating out of her chest. She knew the next few minutes would completely change her life.

"There's something I want to talk to you about..." Persia started.

"No, please let me speak first. I need to get this out. It won't take long." Jade looked at the ground. Persia was worried, so she just nodded. "I have spent a lot of time thinking about what I want and need. I don't feel any type of security in our relationship. You go off publicly with these other women; my family and friends are looking at me crazy. I'm looking at myself crazy..."

"I know Jade, but look..." Persia cut her off.

"Please, Persia. Don't cut me off. I have to get this out." Jade didn't look at Persia; she continued to look at the ground. "I know what I want, and I can't ask you to change who you are to try to give it to me. I love you." Jade finally looked Persia in the eye. "I'm just not in love with you anymore. It's time for us to go our separate ways."

"What?" Persia was stunned.

"We have stayed right with each other. The only times we weren't with each other were at work and when we were with our other lovers. This time without you...I was with Jayden. A lot has changed for me during this week, and I just don't think we are a good fit anymore. Jayden is ready to give me what I am looking for, and I'm falling in love with him." Tears ran down Jade's face. "Goodbye, Persia." Jade turned away.

"Wait!" Don't walk away, I understand. You know what...I don't...I don't want to keep you here." Persia lied as she grabbed Jade by the waist. Her caramel skin spun Persia into the past and almost into begging.

"What Persia! I've said what I had to say. Now let me go!" Jade reluctantly requested.

"You're right; you've said what you had to say. But no, you will listen to what I have to say." The tension fell out of Jade's body, allowing her to comply with the request laid in front of her. She indulged in the strength of Persia's hold and didn't move.

"You say you know what you want, and he is what you want. I can respect that, but I must let you know...He will never make your body move the way I did. How did you get on the tip of your toes to make sure the smallest amount of air was not between us? The way your back arched when I grazed my nail down the middle of it. The way your head went limp and your eyes closed from my breath, the tip of my lip nearing the steepest slope of your neck, the anticipation causing your breathing to slow down, get deeper, longer...just like right now."

Jade broke free from the warm, arousing embrace of her former lover. Her mind raced at high speeds because, in the deepest part of her heart, she knew Persia was reading her soul.

"Women want to be with that man that loves them poetically, so they can take that one last deep breath and let go; let go of their fears, inhibitions, worries. While you, on the other hand, are in denial," Persia continued.

Jade's head fell in embarrassment. Persia knew her better than anyone.

"You fail to realize that you're not waiting to exhale; you're in denial about the fact that you already have. You're not waiting for the perfect man; you're running from this perfect woman. This woman who has made you exhale every time we hugged, every time I ran my lips across yours, every time I whispered, I love you in your ear. Look. Jade, I'm not trying to make you stay; you don't belong here...with me. Go back to him, love him. But while he's holding you close and you finally realize that he is not what you want, don't think of me. Don't call me, don't write me, don't text me, don't IM me, don't tweet me. Just let me be. You were my caramel, and I don't have a sweet tooth anymore." Persia grazed Jade's face while tears continued to run down her cheeks.

This love was like no other. She knew that one day, while Jade allowed this man to make love to her, she would think of the times they had, the love they made, the love she lost. Her heart cried for Jade, but she knew she had to move on. "I was going to give it all up for you."

Jade broke free of Persia's grasp, stared at the ground, and walked to her car. With every step made and every tear dropped, Jade swallowed her love for Persia and hid it deep where no one would ever find it. She knew Persia would never understand why she had to do this. Why she had to protect her?

Persia stood there in disbelief. She was ready to change everything for Jade, and therefore, she wanted to talk to Persia. She allowed her body to relax and sat on a swing. *Damn, Lexi is waiting on me.* She quickly jumped into her car and headed back towards the hotel. She sent a quick text to Karen, letting her know Jade had dumped her and that she would fill her in soon.

"Well, well, well, late Larry," Lexi answered the door wearing a black corset, black lace boy shorts, and six-inch heels. Persia took in every inch of her.

"My apologies for being tardy. Forgive me," Persia apologized. Lexi stepped back and allowed her into the room. There were roses everywhere, champagne chilling, and an array of fruit on the table.

"I guess you're fine," Lexi teased as she led Persia to the couch.

"I don't want to be a downer, but we should talk," Persia stated.

"Awe, don't be a Donald Downer," Lexi pleaded.

"I just need to talk." Persia looked Lexi in her eyes. Lexi could see something was going on.

"Oh, Zaddi. Talk to me. What's going on?" Lexi asked as she grabbed Persia's hand.

"Jade and I are done. She decided she wanted to be with Jayden," Persia said.

"I'm sorry, baby." Lexi was sincere; she knew what Jade meant to Persia. She couldn't help but feel relieved.

"Don't be sorry. She did the right thing for her and me both. She needs monogamy, and I don't. I do want to ask you something," Persia paused.

"Spit it out." Lexi was intrigued.

Chapter Twelve

Jade sat in her car and watched Persia as she sat on the swing. She waited for Persia to get into her car and pull off before she left. *Persia would never understand why we couldn't be together, and I wish it were my place to tell her about me and Jayden. He would kill me if I did that.*

"Hey there," Jade answered her phone.

"I'm on the way home. I want you to be there when I get there. Did you pick up the rest of your things?" Jayden asked.

"Yes, I did. I have the last batch in the car now, and I'm on my way home. I will see you there," Jade responded.

"Did you talk to Persia?" Jayden asked.

"Yes, I did. We are done." Jade answered.

"And Alex?" he continued.

"I told her we couldn't be friends for a while, as you said." Jade quickly answered his questions without hesitation.

"OK. Cashmere will be at the house when you get there. I told her to go into her room and wait for me, so don't engage until I get there," Jayden demanded.

"Yes, Jayden. I miss you and can't wait to see you," Jade purred.

"I can't wait to see you. See you soon." Jayden hung up.

Jade rushed to her new home. She didn't bother to get anything out of her car. *I missed Cashmere so much. I must see her before Jayden gets home.* She went straight to Cashmere's room. Cashmere was coming out of her bathroom with only a towel wrapped around her waist.

"What are you doing here?" Cashmere was startled.

"Listen. Jayden will be home soon. I want you before he gets here," Jade demanded.

"I won't be ready when he gets here." Cashmere tried to put up a fight, but her towel was already on the ground. She quietly complied.

Fifteen minutes later, the front door opened, interrupting Jade and Cashmere. Cashmere rushed into the bathroom. Jade wiped her face with Cashmere's towel and went to meet Jayden.

"There you are." He smiled. She welcomed him home with a kiss. He could smell Cashmere's scent on her face.

"You know I don't like to be disobeyed," Jayden stated. Jade stepped back. She could feel his mood change. "I told you not to interact with Cashmere until I got here. You disobeyed me." Jayden lifted Jade's chin and kissed, gently sucking on her bottom lip.

"I'm sorry." Jade apologized.

"I know." Jayden smiled. "Cashmere, come here." Cashmere rushed into the room, fully dressed in her assigned lingerie.

"Yes?" she asked.

"Get dressed. Our time is canceled for the night." Jayden kissed Cashmere's forehead, grabbed Jade's hand, and went to the bedroom. Jade and Cashmere lingered on each other until they couldn't see each other anymore. "Get undressed. It's time for your punishment."

"Yes, sir," Jade smirked.

71

Chapter Thirteen

"Don't be sorry. She did the right thing for her and me both. She needs monogamy, and I don't. I do want to ask you something," Persia paused. Lexi waited for her to continue.

"Spit it out." Lexi was impatiently intrigued. She had a big surprise for Persia, which was the reason for the hotel room.

"Lexi..." Persia held Lexi's hands. "...I was a fool. I looked for my primary in the wrong woman, and the right one was sitting in front of me the whole time." Lexi's heart started beating out of her chest. She knew what was coming next.

"I want to take that step with you," Persia stated. Lexi was cautiously excited. She didn't know exactly what Persia meant, but she knew they may be thinking the same thing.

"Can I tell you my surprise first?" Lexi asked. She wanted to make sure when Persia asked her question, she knew where her mindset was.

"Sure." Persia had a perplexed look on her face. It amused Lexi.

"I know I have worked a lot over the last year. I didn't want to be away from you as much as I was, but I needed to do some things. My job promoted me, which means I am going to travel less and work from my home office." Lexi showed her excitement.

"Congratulations! I'm proud of you," Persia responded.

"Thank you." Lexi hugged Persia. *I love her so much.* "I wasn't ready to commit to anything with anyone because of my work schedule. Now that has changed, I'm ready to move forward with you." Lexi held her breath for a moment until a smile spread across Persia's face. "What did you have to say to me?"

"Alexis, I want to move to the next stage. Let's make us official." Persia smiled. Lexi wanted to jump out of her skin but had to maintain her composure. She wasn't going to let Persia see how happy she was.

"You know I don't need anyone else. If I'm your primary, I'm fine with your other lovers." Lexi straddled Persia. She watched Persia's eyes trace her chocolate curves. It turned her on to see Persia's attraction to her.

"For now, it's just your and my vanilla thickness," Persia assured Lexi. Lexi really didn't hear much about Persia's other lover. She always told Lexi their relationship was strictly sexual. *I will have to get Persia to bring her to meet me. I can't have any of her lovers misunderstanding our situation.* "I want a closed triad. Just something to think about."

"And I will definitely think about it; maybe you'll be lucky enough to have me choose her," Lexi said playfully. She knew a few ladies that would make a great fit for them, but for now, she would enjoy her king. "Ready for a bath, my King?"

"I am." Lexi led Persia to the whirlpool tub full of bubbles and roses.

That night, Lexi allowed herself to let go of her inhibitions while Persia made love to her for what felt like the first time.

Persia thought she was addicted to caramel...but it's always the melting chocolate that will have them licking their fingers for more.

A Word from the Author

Thank you so much for reading Soror Love! This is just the beginning of the Nu Nu Lambda series and the Nu Delta Xi series. If you enjoyed this story, could you leave a review? Make sure to follow for updates and exclusives!
Instagram and Tiktok - @AuthorPhree

Did you love *Caramel Addiction*? Then you should read *Her Mother, My Love*[1] by Shaun J. Phree!

In the spellbinding pages of "Her Mother My Love," acclaimed author Shaun J. Phree weaves a tale of love, redemption, and the indomitable spirit of human connection.

Meet Dana, a resilient 21-year-old African American lesbian stud, whose life takes an unexpected turn when she finds herself without a home after years as a devoted live-in nanny for a wealthy family. Seeking solace in her best friend and ex-girlfriend

---

1. https://books2read.com/u/bxBzzJ

2. https://books2read.com/u/bxBzzJ

from high school, Perri, Dana's life takes a surprising twist when she meets Andrea, a 19-year-old single mother with a captivating 3-year-old daughter, Trisha.

As Dana embraces her role as Trisha's nanny, a profound bond forms between them, leading to a heartfelt exploration of love and self-discovery. However, as the plot unfolds, hidden secrets and long-suppressed emotions come to the surface, setting the stage for a captivating tale of May-December love.

In the midst of this intricate web of relationships, Dana finds herself drawn to Connie, Andrea's mother, a pillar of love and support in their lives. As Dana and Connie cautiously build their relationship in secret, Perri's unspoken love for Dana simmers, adding a layer of complexity to the story.

"Her Mother My Love" delves into the raw emotions of love and family, navigating the complexities of life with authenticity and tenderness. Shaun J. Phree's masterful storytelling weaves a narrative that resonates long after the final page.

Experience the power of love's transformative journey in this heartwarming tale that celebrates diverse voices and explores the true essence of human connections. As secrets unravel and emotions collide, readers are taken on an unforgettable rollercoaster of emotions.

Unlock the captivating pages of "Her Mother My Love" and immerse yourself in a story that will touch your heart and leave you yearning for more.

"A tale of love, resilience, and the intricacies of family bonds that will stay with you long after you close the book."

www.ingramcontent.com/pod-product-compliance
Lightning Source LLC
Chambersburg PA
CBHW050759160726
48004CB00002B/631